Lottie and Dottie Sow Sunflowers

There are lots of Early Reader stories you might enjoy.

Look at the back of the book or, for a complete list, visit www.orionbooks.co.uk

Lottie and Dottie Sow Sunflowers

By Claire Burgess

Illustrated by
Marijke van Veldhoven

Orion
Children's Books

First published in Great Britain in 2015
by Orion Children's Books
an imprint of the Hachette Children's Book Group
published by Hodder and Stoughton
Orion House
5 Upper Saint Martin's Lane
London WC2H 9EA
An Hachette UK company

1 3 5 7 9 10 8 6 4 2

ISBN 978 1 4440 1469 3

A catalogue record for this book is available from the British Library.

Printed and bound in China

www.orionchildrensbooks.co.uk

For my Mum, who gave me my first patch of soil to grow my seeds in, thank you!
C.B.

To Ronnie, the best support I could wish for.
M.v.V.

This is Lottie and this is her little
sister, Dottie. Lottie and Dottie
love growing things.

It was a lovely sunny day and
Lottie, Dottie and Mum were
looking round Mr McWelly's
garden centre.

Dottie saw a poster with lots of sunflowers on it.

"It's a competition," said Mr McWelly. "Would you like to enter?"
"Yes, please," said Dottie.

"Can I grow a *huge* sunflower?" asked Dottie.
"Yes," said Mr McWelly. "Good luck!"

"Thank you," said Dottie.

When Lottie and Dottie got home they went into the garden and opened the bag.

Inside they found

a packet of seeds,

two small pots,

a small bag of soil,

two labels,

a pen,

a small bag
of stones,

and a list
of what
to do.

Lottie and Dottie read the instructions.

"First we need the pots,"
said Lottie.

"Next we need to fill them
with soil."

"Now pat the soil down, but not too much."

"What's next?" asked Dottie.
"Next we get the seeds!" said
Lottie.
Dottie found the seeds in the bag.
"They're so pretty," she said.
"They look just like the sun."

Dottie opened the packet very carefully. She didn't want to drop any seeds.

"How many are there?" asked Lottie.

Dottie counted, "One . . . two."

"That's one for each pot," said Lottie.

"Now we need to cover the seeds with a bit more soil," said Lottie.

Then Dottie watered them.

"Can I do the labels?" asked Dottie.
"Yes," said Lottie.
So Dottie put one label in each
pot.

She put the pots on her bedroom
window sill, so that she could
watch them grow.

After a week Dottie noticed that the soil on the top had moved. "They're starting to grow," said Lottie. "They will be popping through the soil soon."

A couple of days later, Dottie saw
two little green plants.
"Lottie, look!" she said.

As the sun shone,
the green plants grew bigger

and bigger

and bigger.

Dottie watched them every day.
As they grew she painted pictures
of them and stuck them on her
bedroom wall.

Soon the sunflowers grew too big
for their pots.

"We need to plant them outside,"
said Lottie. "Let's do one today
and one tomorrow."

Dottie carried one plant into
the garden.
"Where shall we plant it?"
she asked.
"Over here by the fence,"
said Lottie.

As Lottie and Dottie dug, a face
popped over the fence. It was
Basil, the little boy from next door.

Basil watched as they put some
water in the bottom of the hole.

Dottie took the pot off the plant.

Then she planted the sunflower in the hole.

Lottie and Dottie smoothed the soil around the sunflower, and patted it down.

The next morning Dottie went
to see her sunflower. But she
couldn't find it.
"Where is it?" she asked Lottie.

They looked and looked, but it
had gone.
Dottie started to cry.
"Someone has taken it," she said.

Mum came to see what was wrong.

"It's been eaten by a snail,"
Mum said.
"Oh no!" said Dottie.

"Do you have another sunflower plant?" asked Mum.
"Yes," said Dottie and ran to get it.

Mum asked Lottie to get the bag of stones.

They planted the second
sunflower.
"Don't forget to use the stones
this time," said Mum.
"They're very pointy," said
Dottie.

"Now your sunflower will be safe," said Mum.

As the weeks went by the
sunflower got taller and taller.
It grew and grew.

Then it grew some more.

As it got bigger and bigger they
watered it more and more.

Soon they had to tie it to the
fence to stop it from falling over.

Then it was as tall as Mum.
"Wow!" said Basil.

"When is the flower going to open?" asked Dottie.
"I don't know," said Lottie.

Still the sunflower grew. The stem got thicker and the leaves got bigger. And it kept on growing.

Then one morning, something magical happened.

"My sunflower has opened,"
said Dottie.

Later that day Mr McWelly came to measure it. He had to stand on a long ladder to reach the top.

The next day Mum showed
them the newspaper. There on
the front page was the picture
of Lottie and Dottie. They had
grown the tallest sunflower.

Dottie put the picture on her bedroom wall. "Let's grow an even bigger sunflower next year!" she said.

How to Grow Sunflowers

Sow your sunflower seeds in
April or May.

Soon they will begin to grow.

Plant them outside in June.

Make sure you keep them safe from snails.

If they grow really tall they may
need support.

Water the plants well to help
them grow.

Keep a record of how tall your sunflower grows.

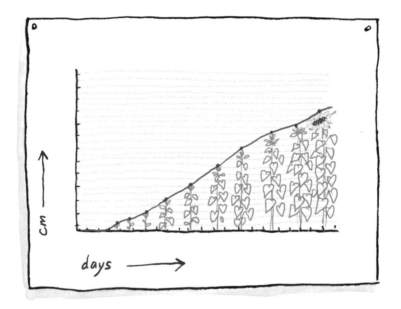

What are you going to read next?

Have more adventures with Horrid Henry,

or save the day with Anthony Ant!

Become a superhero with Monstar,

float off to sea with Algy,

or have your very own Pirates' Picnic.

Grow carrots with

Lottie and Dottie,

make magic with
The Witch Dog,

and cast a
spell with

The Three
Little Magicians.

Enjoy all the Early Readers.